NUESTRO AUTOBÚS
THE BUS FOR US

Suzanne Bloom

Translated by Aída E. Marcuse

Boyds Mills Press
Honesdale, Pennsylvania

Text and illustrations copyright © 2001 by Suzanne Bloom
Spanish translation copyright © 2008 by Boyds Mills Press
All rights reserved

Boyds Mills Press, Inc.
815 Church Street
Honesdale, Pennsylvania 18431
Printed in China

The Library of Congress has cataloged the English hardcover edition as follows:

Bloom, Suzanne.
The bus for us / written and illustrated by Suzanne Bloom.—1st ed.
[32]p.: col. ill. ; cm.
Summary: On her first day of school, Tess wonders what the school bus will look like.
ISBN-13: 978-1-56397-932-3
ISBN-10: 1-56397-932-2
1. School — Fiction. 2. School buses — Fiction. I. Title.
[E]   21   2001   AC   CIP
00-102348
Bilingual (Spanish-English) Paperback ISBN: 978-1-59078-629-1

First bilingual (Spanish-English) edition, 2008
The text of this book is set in Palatino.

10 9 8 7 6 5 4 3 2

To four fabulous first-grade teachers and to Alice, who always asked
—S.B.

¿Es éste nuestro autobús, Gus?

Is this the bus for us, Gus?

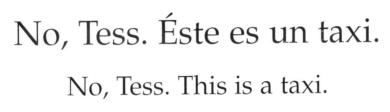

No, Tess. Éste es un taxi.

No, Tess. This is a taxi.

¿Es éste nuestro autobús, Gus?

Is this the bus for us, Gus?

No, Tess. Ésta es una grúa.

No, Tess. This is a tow truck.

¿Es éste nuestro autobús, Gus?

Is this the bus for us, Gus?

No, Tess. Éste es un camión de bomberos.

No, Tess. This is a fire engine.

¿Es éste nuestro autobús, Gus?

Is this the bus for us, Gus?

No. Tess. Éste es un camión de helados.

No, Tess. This is an ice-cream truck.

¿Es éste nuestro autobús, Gus?

Is this the bus for us, Gus?

No, Tess. Éste es un camión de la basura.

No, Tess. This is a garbage truck.

¿Es éste nuestro autobús, Gus?

Is this the bus for us, Gus?

No, Tess. Ésta es una excavadora.

No, Tess. This is a backhoe.

¿Es éste nuestro autobús, Gus?

Is this the bus for us, Gus?

Sí, Tess. Éste es nuestro autobús. ¡Vamos!

Yes, Tess. This is the bus for us. Let's go!

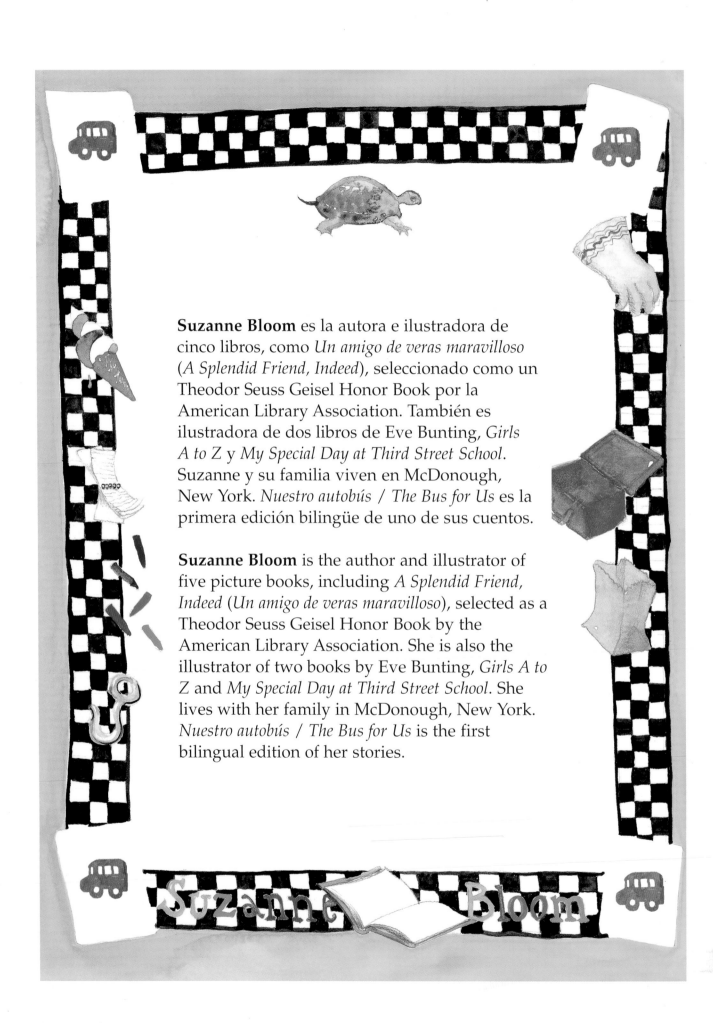

Suzanne Bloom es la autora e ilustradora de cinco libros, como *Un amigo de veras maravilloso* (*A Splendid Friend, Indeed*), seleccionado como un Theodor Seuss Geisel Honor Book por la American Library Association. También es ilustradora de dos libros de Eve Bunting, *Girls A to Z* y *My Special Day at Third Street School*. Suzanne y su familia viven en McDonough, New York. *Nuestro autobús / The Bus for Us* es la primera edición bilingüe de uno de sus cuentos.

Suzanne Bloom is the author and illustrator of five picture books, including *A Splendid Friend, Indeed* (*Un amigo de veras maravilloso*), selected as a Theodor Seuss Geisel Honor Book by the American Library Association. She is also the illustrator of two books by Eve Bunting, *Girls A to Z* and *My Special Day at Third Street School*. She lives with her family in McDonough, New York. *Nuestro autobús / The Bus for Us* is the first bilingual edition of her stories.